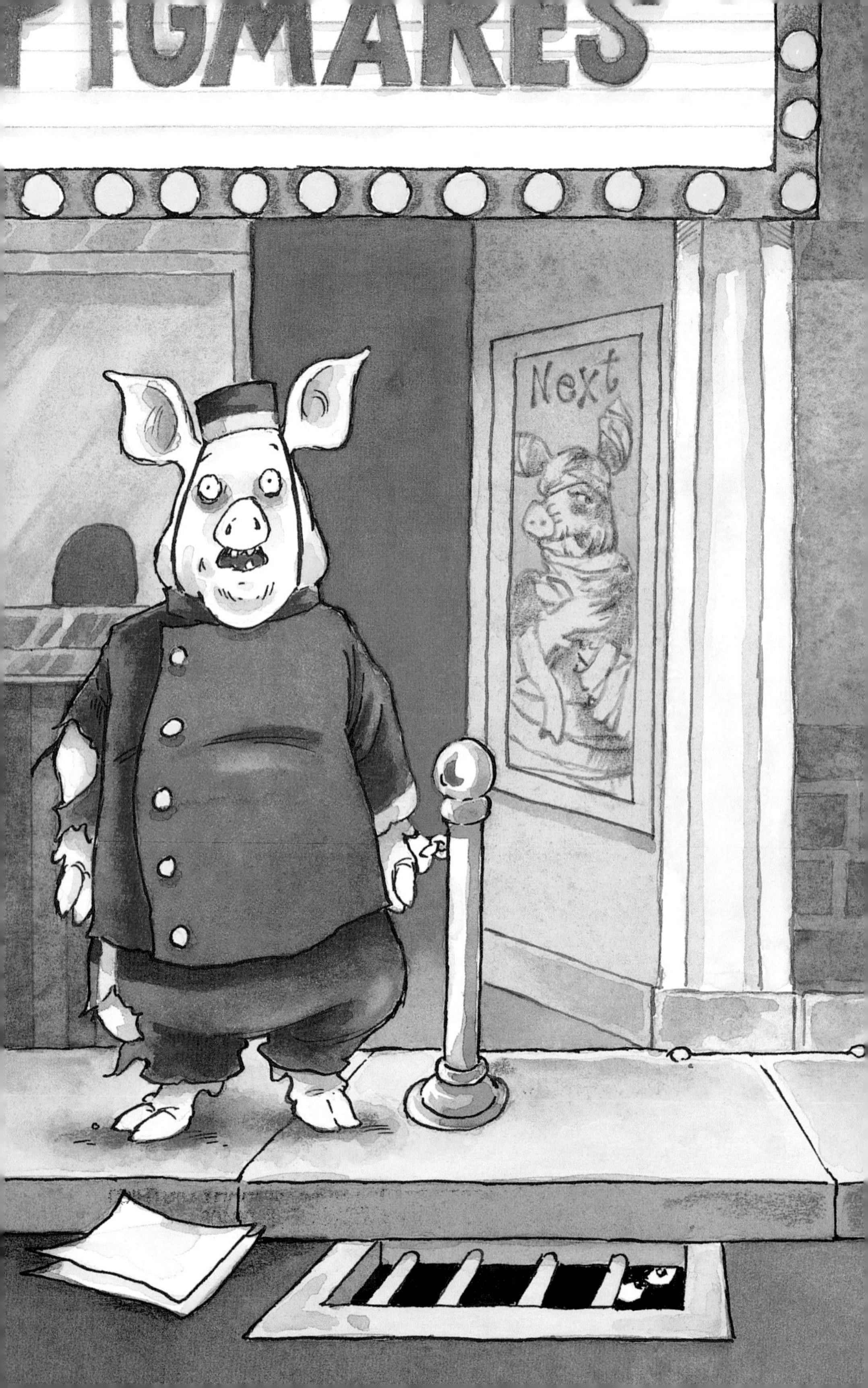

IGMARES
Next

DOUG CUSHMAN

PIGMARES

Porcine Poems of the Silver Screen

ioi Charlesbridge

Table of Contents

Pigmares

A thousand-foot pig breathing nuclear fire.
Gurgling gasps from a swamp's murky mire.
Sharp fangs and red eyes on pale porcine faces.
Dead zombies crawl out from foul-smelling places.
Vampire pigs fly from castles at night;
their silver wings glow in the ghostly moonlight.
An ice-covered monster crawls out of a cave.
A creature made whole out of parts from a grave.
A mummified swine puts a curse on my head—
I should *never* watch monsters on film before bed!

Frankenswine

Like an old crazy quilt, I'm pieces and parts
from nine different bodies and five different hearts.
My brain is a poet's, my snout's from a thief,
my hooves all belonged to the old fire chief.
I'm slogging through swamps and mist-covered bogs,
hunted by farmers with torches and dogs.
Through mountains and towns, over oceans and snow,
I've ended up here on this Arctic ice floe.
So I sit here alone at the world's frozen end,
just looking for someone whom I can call friend.

The Mummy Pig

I once was a pharaoh, a mighty king,
who ruled the length of the Nile.
I bowed to Horus, the great falcon god,
as well as the crocodile.

One hundred dung beetles, the scarabs of Ra,
now crawl from my snout and ears.
I open my eyes and awake in this tomb
from my sleep of three thousand years.

My tomb holds fine gifts of diamonds and gold
and my robe of rich golden thread.
Some magical spells on an old paper scroll—
this book brings life to the dead!

I rise from inside my sarcophagus tomb
to breathe in the life-giving plants,
then wander the world to put curses on those
who put sand in my underpants.

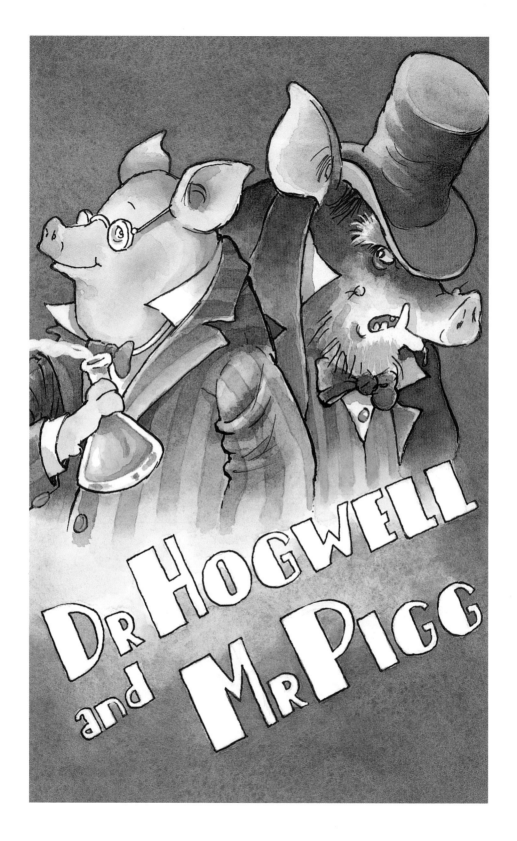

Dr. Hogwell and Mr. Pigg

I'm mild Dr. Hogwell,
friend to all in town.
I heal the sick and helpless.
I'm a pig of wide renown.

**I'm Mr. Pigg, the monster,
a swine too ugly to behold.
I'm vicious, mean, and savage.
My blood runs icy cold.**

My potions help the ailing.
I dispense them with great pride.
But one I give to no one—
it's a secret I must hide.

**I walk the streets of Paris,
hunting victims every night.
I snort, then steal their purses.
They scream in ghastly fright.**

The potion I created
burns my throat and curls my hair.
This revolting, gross concoction
tastes like dirty underwear.

**The changes happen quickly.
I grow fangs that reach my snout.
I spit and fart and belch—
city folks, look out!**

I feel so weird and different,
**I'm split in half, you see.
Who's that in the mirror?**
Is that Mr. Pigg . . . or me?

The Phantom
Hog of the Opera

The Phantom Hog
of the Opera

Beneath the old opera
in a dark catacomb
an organ drones low
with a sonorous tone.
Deep reverberations
shake the seats and stalls.
They rattle the scenery
and boom through the halls.

The Phantom is playing,
scribbling tunes for his play,
a sad tale of pig love
for his sweetheart Renée.
He sings the last word
of his tragic libretto.
The music is done.
His opera—*Pigoletto!*

The Werehog

A silver moon is rising
over distant hills.
A howling breaks the quiet night
and shakes the windowsills.
Piglets, piglets—lock your doors
and shut the windows tight!
A shadow moves along the moors—
the werehog howls tonight!

Why *is* the werehog howling?
Is his pig swill at an end?
Did he stub his toe upon a rock
or lose his best pig friend?
The werehog howls his torment.
He yowls his mournful tune.
The saddest sound you'll ever hear:
his oinking at the moon!

Piglets of the Night

In eastern Pigsylvania
there's a castle made of stone.
It's dark, cold, and foreboding.
No one seems to be at home.
But when the daylight disappears
and a pale, gray moon shines bright,
squeals cut through the darkness.
It's the Piglets of the Night!

Little vampire piglets
walk the night with hungry eyes
or sometimes change to bat-pigs
to hunt in moonlit skies.
Will they visit me at bedtime
as I'm eating up my slops—
flying through an open window,
licking fang-toothed chops?
I wonder, will they tell me,
"Calm yourself! Be still!
Ve don't vant to drink your blood!
Ve just vant to drink your swill!"?

The Invisible Swine

I squeezed the juice from cottage cheese.
I added pepper (which made me sneeze),
pickle juice, some chicken necks,
one tablespoon of Element X.
I drank it down; it was soon apparent
I wasn't there! I was *transparent!*

I loved to play all kinds of tricks,
like scaring friends with floating bricks,
or wearing pants or underwear
to make it seem they walked on air.
I rattled doors and cooking pots,
then tied the bath towels into knots.

Now no one wants to come and play.
They've packed their bags and gone away.
So I sit here in this empty place.
I have no friends . . .
and I miss my face.

Earth vs.
the Flying Sausage

We came from Planet Pigzon, a tiny star in space.

We came with flashing ray guns to destroy the human race.

With brains the size of Neptune, and telepathic thought,

we came to conquer Earth with a vile and evil plot.

Our planet's slowly dying; our world is almost dead.

We need a brand-new planet to keep our pig race fed!

We came in flying saucers shaped like spinning sausage links.

We burned the Tower of Pisa and burned the silent Sphinx.

We burned the Eiffel Tower. We burned old Harvard Square.

We fried the governor's house in the state of Delaware.

We made the redwood forests a mighty conflagration,

then burned the pizza palaces to paralyze your nation!

But now we are defeated; our spaceships lie forsaken.

You fried our sausage saucers and turned us all to bacon!

Porker from the Black Lagoon

In the muddy, murky Black Lagoon
a creature floats and waits
with scaly claws and slimy snout
and breath that nauseates.
It gargles, groans, gurgles, gasps,
and burbles bubbly burps.
It nibbles fish heads, sucks their bones,
and belches as it slurps.
It's grouchy, and it grumbles gripes
in effervescent snorts.
It's hard to grin when every day
there's water in your shorts.

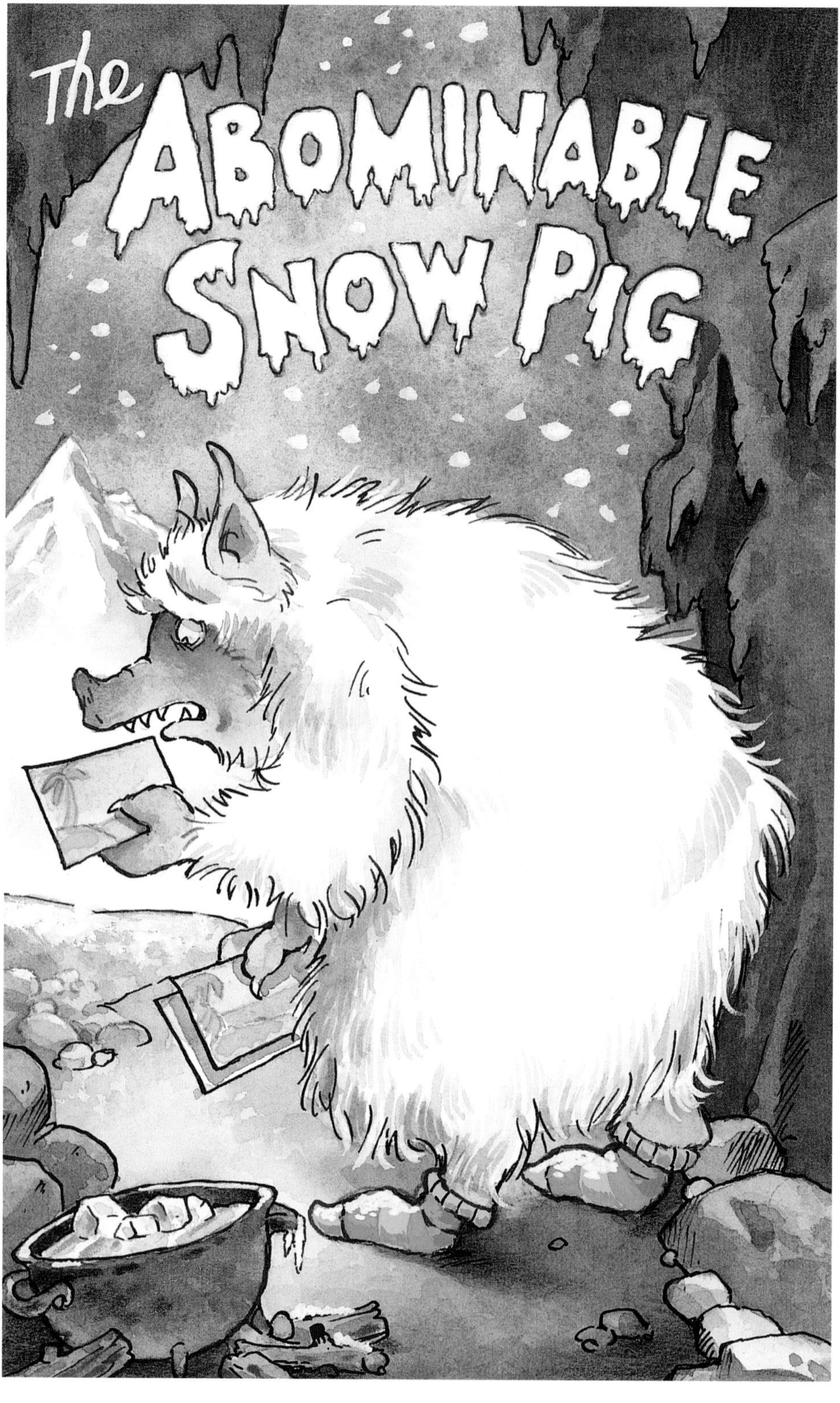
The
ABOMINABLE
SNOW PIG

The Abominable Snow Pig

On a high, frozen mountain
in a range in Tibet,
the ice and snow wail
in a sub-zero duet.
My cave is ice covered,
and so is my stew.
My hands are like ice cubes.
My feet have turned blue.
There's snow in the pantry
and frost on my socks.
The logs in my chimney
are giant ice blocks.
I shiver and shake
as the howling wind screeches
and look through my postcards
of tropical beaches.

The Bride of Frankenswine

A wooden table with a squeaking crank

holds a shrouded form near a bubbling tank.

The howling wind drives the pounding rain.

A rattling *clank* sounds from a rusted chain.

The crazy doctor pulls a switch—

the covered form starts to shake and twitch.

Thunder crashes in the rain-soaked skies.

"It lives! It LIVES!" the doctor cries.

One ear quivers, . . . then . . . another.

She jerks one hoof, then moves another.

The monster opens her glowing eyes.

She groans just once and starts to rise.

The wooden table begins to creak.

The monster moans, then starts to speak.

"I want the truth," declares the bride.

"Is Frankie cute? Or should I hide?"

Pigzilla

Born undersea from toxic waste,
miles from Tokyo's shore,
I'm a scaly beast below the waves,
with a radioactive roar.
I blow smoke rings through my nostrils;
my eyes glow ruby red.
My breath is fire, with white-hot flames
that melt concrete and lead.
I'm really not an evil beast
as I slumber in the deep,
but all you noisy townsfolk
disturb my peaceful sleep.
So, *please,* could you be quiet?
Maybe then I'll leave your coast.
But if you don't, I guarantee
I'll turn your town to toast.

Day of the Pigweed

We're alien seeds from deep outer space;
we arrived on a comet's bright tail.
Your warm, cozy Earth feels good to our roots—
our foul purpose it's time to unveil.
We've come here to plant our alien race
and spread our vines far and wide.
We're pig-eating plants from Galaxy X.
There's nowhere to run to or hide.
We're Creepers of Fear, cosmic Pigweed from Space.
Through our stalks runs green chlorophyll.
Wrapping our tendrils 'round helpless fat pigs,
we'll gobble you all and your swill.
We'll conquer your Earth with green creeping vines
and indulge our taste for fine pork.

What is that strange, hungry gleam in your eyes?
Is that dressing? And a large salad fork?

Pig Kong

I hear the beat of jungle drums
and a deep sonorous gong.
The festival begins again
for *me*—the great Pig Kong!

I protect them from all monsters,
from beasts both large and strong,
from snake to stegosaurus.
They worship *me*—the great Pig Kong!

A goat, some fish, a chicken,
a sow in a pink sarong—
They offer up their sacrifice
to feed the great Pig Kong!

I cannot take their offerings;
I'm not a gross barbarian.
All that meat and fish and fowl—
I'm Kong the Vegetarian!

The Legend of Sleepy Wallow

I was once an honest beggar
who asked for crusts of bread.
I disappeared one evening
and was found . . . without a head.
I ride through Sleepy Wallow
on Hellcat, black as night,
then toward the open country
as the townsfolk scream in fright.
My steed has eyes of fire
that glow like molten lead.
I scour homes and graveyards
for my beloved missing head.
I ride along the highway,
a demonic, devilish bat.
'Tisn't just a head I want,
but a place to put my hat.

Night of the Living Ham

Crawling out from cold, damp graves,
they push tombstones to one side.
With vacant eyes they stare ahead,
their cold mouths open wide.
They snort and grunt dull, guttural sounds.
Something's hanging from a snout.
Decomposing bones detach;
worms and maggots crawl about.
They stumble on decaying limbs;
flesh hangs like half-pulled toffee.
They look just like my Ma and Pa—
before their morning coffee!

Movie Credits

Frankenswine
Inspired by Mary Shelley's novel *Frankenstein,* published in 1818. The most familiar image of the monster is from the 1931 film starring Boris Karloff, directed by James Whale.

The Mummy Pig
There have been many tales of mummies' curses, the most famous being the series of mishaps that followed the opening of King Tutankhamen's tomb in 1922. The classic image of a mummy comes from the 1932 film *The Mummy,* starring Boris Karloff. Interestingly the mummy itself was on screen for less than a minute.

Dr. Hogwell and Mr. Pigg
Based on the novella *Strange Case of Dr. Jekyll and Mr. Hyde,* written by Robert Louis Stevenson and published in 1886. There have been many film versions of the story; one of the earliest was a silent film starring John Barrymore in 1920.

The Phantom Hog of the Opera
Inspired by the 1925 silent film *The Phantom of the Opera,* starring Lon Chaney Sr. The story was originally published as *Le Fantôme de l'Opera,* serialized in France by Gaston Leroux from 1909 to 1910. The *Pigoletto* reference in the poem is a nod to the famous opera *Rigoletto,* written by Guiseppe Verdi in 1851.

The Werehog
There are many stories of werewolves around the world. Perhaps the most iconic image is seen in *The Wolf Man* (1941), starring Lon Chaney Jr.

Piglets of the Night

There are many stories and tales of vampires from around the world. The best known is *Dracula,* written by Bram Stoker in 1897. Popular images of the vampire come from the German silent film *Nosferatu* (1922) and *Dracula* (1931), the latter starring Béla Lugosi. In the 1931 film, after hearing a wolf howl, Dracula says, "Listen to them. Children of the night! What music they make."

The Invisible Swine

Inspired by H. G. Wells's *The Invisible Man,* serialized and published as a novella in 1897. A film based on the book was released in 1933 and starred Claude Rains.

Earth vs. the Flying Sausage

Inspired by the 1956 film *Earth vs. the Flying Saucers,* directed by Fred F. Sears. The special effects were designed by Ray Harryhausen, considered by many to be one of the masters of stop-motion filmmaking.

Porker from the Black Lagoon

Inspired by the 1954 film *Creature from the Black Lagoon,* directed by Jack Arnold. The film was originally released in 3-D, a new technology at the time. There were two sequels.

The Abominable Snow Pig

Based on the yeti, a legendary creature living in the Himalayas. "Yeti" is derived from the Tibetan compound word *yeh-teh,* which is roughly translated as "rock bear." There are not many movies featuring the yeti, which is also known as the abominable snowman. The low-budget film *The Snow Creature* (1954) is considered the first.

The Bride of Frankenswine

Inspired in part by Mary Shelley's *Frankenstein*. A popular image of the monster is actress Elsa Lanchester's portrayal in director James Whale's film *Bride of Frankenstein* (1935).

Pigzilla

Inspired by the famous Japanese monster Godzilla, first appearing in the film *Gojira* (Godzilla) in 1954. Godzilla is a *daikaiju,* which is translated as "giant monster."

Day of the Pigweed

There are many movies that feature man-eating plants. Two well-known films are *The Little Shop of Horrors* (first filmed in 1960, then made into a musical and filmed again in 1986) and *The Day of the Triffids* (1962).

Pig Kong

Inspired by the 1933 film *King Kong,* in which the title character, a giant ape, is brought to New York City and meets his end atop the Empire State Building. The special effects were designed by Willis O'Brien, who influenced special-effects artists for decades afterward.

The Legend of Sleepy Wallow

Inspired by Washington Irving's short story "The Legend of Sleepy Hollow," first published in 1820. Irving based his story on a German folktale, recorded by Karl Musäus, about a headless horseman. Walt Disney Studios adapted the tale and paired it with a story from *The Wind in the Willows* in the animated film *The Adventures of Ichabod and Mr. Toad* (1949).

Night of the Living Ham

Many stories and movies have been made about zombies, dead creatures that can still move and walk—or lurch—around. The most iconic movie is George A. Romero's *Night of the Living Dead* (1968).

To Jack Prelutsky, not tall or husky,

but a poet to the end.

A rhyming star that plays guitar,

and one whom I call friend.

Copyright © 2012 by Doug Cushman
All rights reserved, including the right of reproduction in whole or in part in any form.
Charlesbridge and colophon are registered trademarks of Charlesbridge Publishing, Inc.

Published by Charlesbridge
85 Main Street
Watertown, MA 02472
(617) 926-0329
www.charlesbridge.com

Library of Congress Cataloging-in-Publication Data
Cushman, Doug.
    Pigmares: porcine poems of the silver screen / Doug Cushman.
        p. cm.
    ISBN 978-1-58089-401-2 (reinforced for library use)
1. Swine—Juvenile poetry. 2. Children's poetry, American. I. Title.
PS3603.U8245P54 2012
811'.6—dc22   2011025703

Printed in Singapore
(hc) 10 9 8 7 6 5 4 3 2 1

Illustrations done in pen and ink and watercolor on French Lanaquarelle watercolor paper
Display type and text type set in Suspicion and Optima
Color separations by KHL Chroma Graphics, Singapore
Printed and bound February 2012 by Imago in Singapore
Production supervision by Brian G. Walker
Designed by Susan Mallory Sherman

The